www.mascotbooks.com

Second printing. This Mascot Books edition printed in 2020.

For more information, please contact:
Mascot Books
620 Herndon Parkway, Suite 320
Herndon, VA 20170
info@mascotbooks.com

Library of Congress Control Number: 2017914807

CPSIA Code: PRT0920B
ISBN-13: 978-1-68401-426-2

Printed in the United States

The Adventures of Forkman

A Children's Book of ETIQUETTE

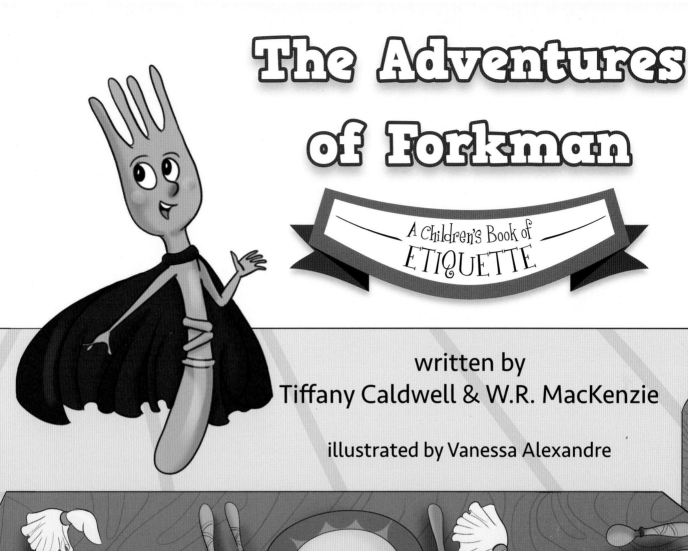

written by
Tiffany Caldwell & W.R. MacKenzie

illustrated by Vanessa Alexandre

Chapter One: Setting the Table

From down the hall, Kathryn and William could hear their mom calling, "Come on, kids! Let's set the table before Dad gets home."

Kathryn and William put their controllers down sadly and got up to make their way to the dining room.

Eager to get back to their video game, Kathryn and William threw the plates and utensils from the cabinet onto the table in a hurry and attempted to sneak away.

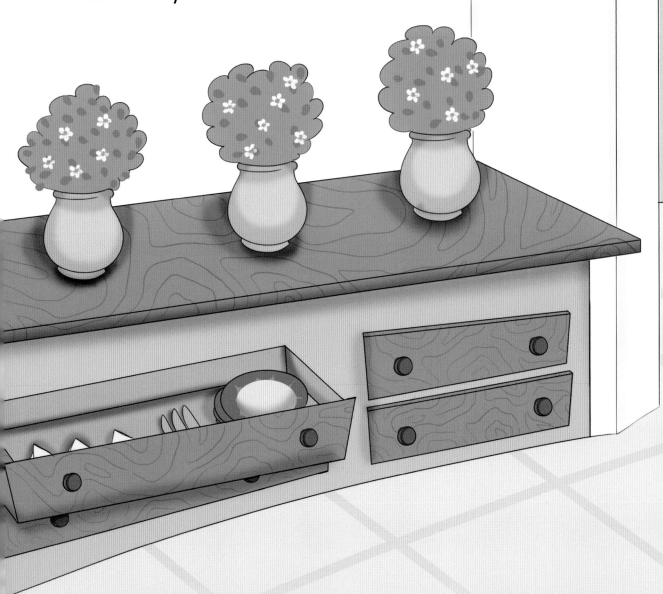

Before they could make an escape, however, they heard an unfamiliar voice behind them say, "Who set this table? Well, I never!"

Kathryn and William slowly turned around to find a fork standing on the table!

"Who are you?" Kathryn exclaimed.

"Hey, kids!" the fork replied excitedly. "My name is Forkman, and I'm going to show you how to properly set the table."

William looked at his sister and then back to Forkman with confusion.

"Let me introduce you to my friends, Spoondude and Knifeguy," Forkman continued.

Suddenly, a spoon and knife on the table by Forkman jumped up to join him with big smiles.

"Kids, would you like to help us set the table?" asked Forkman.

"Okay!" William and Kathryn replied with amusement.

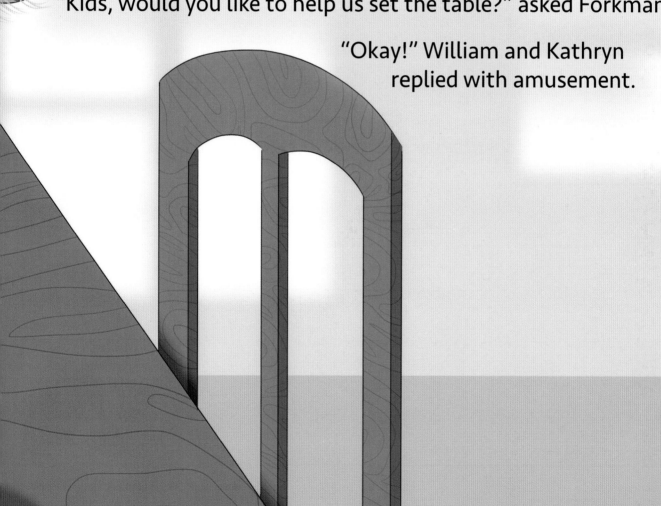

"Well, we're going to need some help from a few more of my friends," Forkman advised.

"Meet Natalie Napkin, Clara Cup, and Pete the Plate," he continued, gesturing to the left of his utensil sidekicks.

"The first step to setting the table is arranging the plate," Forkman began. "Pete goes here!"

The children watched attentively as Forkman directed his friend to his proper spot at the table.

"Next on the table is Natalie Napkin," Forkman continued. "Then, the knife and spoon are placed to the right of the plate."

"And remember, Knifeguy," Forkman cautioned, "You always need to face Pete so your blade doesn't hurt Spoondude!"

"Okay! Let's finish the setting," said Forkman. "After you place the utensils correctly, Clara takes her place above Spoondude and Knifeguy." Forkman looked at the finished setting proudly. "Looks pretty easy, right, kids?"

Kathryn and William responded excitedly, "It sure does!"

"For the finishing touch, I'll take my place to the left of Pete! Why don't you set the rest of the table for Mom and Dad to surprise them?" Forkman asked. "What do you say?"

Kathryn and William smiled as they grabbed the utensils at each end of the table and got to work.

With the table set, Mom and Dad came in with a smile on their faces.

"Kids! The table looks beautiful," Mom exclaimed. "Where did you learn how to do this?"

"Our table friends helped us!" William and Kathryn replied happily.

"Well, we are impressed," Dad said. "How about ice cream for dessert tonight?"

"Yes, please!" the kids exclaimed.

Chapter Two: Cleaning Up

"That ice cream was great!" Kathryn said to her parents as her brother, William, started to sneak away from the table.

"William!" Mom called. "Where do you think you're going?"

"I wanted to go finish playing my game," William pleaded, "... just for a minute!"

"Your dad and I would appreciate it if you and Kathryn would clean up for us tonight before you go back to your video games," Mom said.

Excited to resume their game, Kathryn and William threw their plates and utensils in the sink.

"Come on kids! We can do better than that, don't you think?"

The children stopped in their tracks at the sound of a friend's familiar voice.

"Forkman!" The siblings exclaimed. "Have you come to help us?"

"You bet I have!" Forkman replied.

Eager to learn more from their favorite kitchen friend, Kathryn and William turned to give Forkman their full attention.

"Let's start with clearing the table," Forkman began. "First, we need to put all the food away."

"You're right!" William replied. "If we leave the food out all night, it'll spoil, and we won't have any leftovers for tomorrow."

Kathryn and William grabbed storage containers from the cabinets and started putting the food away. By working together, they were able to put everything away in no time.

"After the food is stored and put away, it's time to take my friends off the table," Forkman instructed.

"William!" Pete said excitedly. "Can you take me to the trash can so I can be cleared off?" William smiled and walked over to the trashcan so he could wipe Pete the Plate clean.

"Much better!" Pete the Plate said with a smile. "It's important that all the food is scraped off so the sink doesn't get stopped up when we get cleaned." While William was busy clearing the plates, Kathryn made sure any leftover liquids in Clara Cup and her friends were poured down the sink.

"What's next, Forkman?" Kathryn and William asked.

"Let's take Natalie Napkin to the laundry room," Forkman said.

"Yes, please! I need to be washed so I can be used next time, " Natalie explained. "By washing the napkins every day, we can reuse them to help keep our planet clean."

After Kathryn and William gathered up Natalie and the other napkins and brought them to the laundry room to be washed, they listened carefully for Forkman's next instruction.

"For the next part," he said with a smile, "you'll need to take Knifeguy and Spoondude to the sink with the other knives and spoons."

Kathryn and William picked up their utensil friends to take them to the sink, but just when they were about to be set down, Knifeguy and Spoondude opened their eyes.

"Wait!" Spoondude exclaimed. "Can you please rinse us off so we don't get sticky?"

Kathryn and William looked at each other and laughed as the utensils enjoyed their quick rinse.

"Is there anything left to do?" Kathryn asked Forkman.

"Just one more step!" Forkman replied. "Have you met Sarah Sponge and Brittney the Broom yet?"

The kids shook their heads until a big smile appeared on the sponge by the sink.

"Sarah!" Forkman exclaimed. "If you put some warm water and soap on her, she will lather up and help wipe the table down."

"Yep!" Sarah said, "And then we need to get Brittney out to sweep up all the bits of food on the floor. We don't want any food left on the floor for critters to get!"

Kathryn and William worked as a team to finish all the things Forkman and his friends asked them to do. When they finished, they put Sarah back by the sink and Brittney back in the closet just before Mom and Dad came back to the kitchen. Everything was done!

"Wow, kids!" Dad exclaimed. "You did great! How did you learn how to do all of this?"

Kathryn and William looked at each other and smiled. "Let's just say we had a little help from some friends."

About the Authors

After thirty-nine years in the bakery business, W.R. MacKenzie felt it was time to share with all children the importance of the family meal and how to properly conduct themselves at a table with characters they could relate to.

Forkman was an idea that came about at the kitchen table with his children when they would talk in a family setting. He would make the fork come alive to explain the proper way to sit at the table for dinner as his four children giggled at the charismatic Forkman. *The Adventures of Forkman* is a way to share these cherished experiences with other children and their families in a fun and educational way.

In 2010, his daughter, Tiffany, approached W.R. to finally write their story. From setting the table to cleaning up after dinner, etiquette is something all children should learn at an early age. Any young family starting out will love these characters and the many lessons they impart throughout their adventures.